SCHOLASTIC JUNIOR CLASSICS

Robinson Crusoe

Daniel Defoe

Retold by Edward W. Dolch, Marguerite P. Dolch,
and Beulah F. Jackson

Illustratred with engravings after designs by J.J. Grandville

New York Toronto London Auckland Sydney
Mexico City New Delhi Hong Kong

ISBN 0-439-23621-5

12 11 10 9 8 7 6 5 4 3   1 2 3 4 5 6/0

Printed in the U.S.A.   40

First Scholastic Trade paperback printing, January 2001

FOREWORD

ONE of the best-loved stories of all time is the tale of Robinson Crusoe, by Daniel Defoe. Every one of us has dreamed of being cast ashore on an island and of what we would do to keep alive and to try to get back to our homes. Exactly such a dream is the fascinating story of Robinson, who spent so many years alone, working with what he had at hand, but who finally was rescued and came home to tell us his great adventure.

As we read of this long stay of Robinson on the island, we are thrilled with fear over his finding of the footprint on the sand, and then thrilled again with his rescue of Friday, and later of still other captives of the cannibals. We are again held in great suspense when we learn that the ship from England is in the power of mutineers who would kill anyone who interfered with them. It is a wonderful story.

The original tale by Daniel Defoe is a long one, full of great detail about Robinson's everyday life. It is hoped that this retelling will give the flavor and sense of reality that the original does and that the reader will then go to the original to enjoy again this great story.

E. W. DOLCH

Urbana, Illinois

Contents

I Am Saved from
the Sea

I WAS born in England in a town beside the sea. I loved the sea and when I was just a boy, I made up my mind that I was going to be a sailor.

When I grew to be a young man, I became a sailor. I had many adventures, but the one I am about to tell you was the greatest adventure of them all.

The ship I was on when this story begins was not a very large ship. There were only fourteen men on board besides the captain, his cabin boy, and myself.

We were sailing near the coast of South America. It was the time of the year when there are very bad storms in that part of the world. They are called hurricanes. All sailors are very much afraid of them.

We had been out of sight of land for many days when our captain told us to get ready for a storm. The sky grew dark and the wind began to blow very hard.

We took down the sails as fast as we could. Before we could get them rolled up, the wind blew so hard that it blew some of the sails away. The big waves began to break over the sides of our ship.

We worked as hard as we could to tie everything down to the deck of the ship. But soon, two of our men were washed overboard when a big wave caught them. The captain ordered us all to go into the cabin, for we could do nothing more.

For twelve days and twelve nights the wind and the rains and the big waves pounded our little ship. Then one morning the wind was still blowing, but not so hard. The captain and some of the sailors carefully opened the door of the cabin and went out on the deck. They had no sooner gotten outside than one man cried, "Land!"

We all ran out of the cabin to look. Just at that minute, the ship struck something and we were all thrown to the deck. A big wave broke over the ship. We had to rush back into the cabin to keep from being washed overboard.

We stood in the cabin looking at one another and thinking that our ship would break apart any minute. We did not know how much longer we had to live. Then our captain said we would try to reach land in our small boats.

On deck, we found that one of our boats had a big hole in it where the wind had driven something through it. But the other boat was still all right. We got it over the side of the ship and all of us that were left got into it.

We were not much better off there than we had been on the ship. The waves lifted us high one minute and dropped us the next. We pulled on our oars as hard as we could.

For a time we seemed to be getting nearer the land. Then a wave as high as a house lifted us, upset our boat, and before I could so much as cry out, I found myself deep in the water!

As I went down, down, down in the rough water, I thought my end had come. But I was a very strong swimmer, and I tried to save myself.

As soon as my head came out of the water, I caught a big breath. Before the next wave broke over me, I saw that I was being carried nearer the shore.

I swam as hard as I could toward the land. Wave after wave lifted me and broke over me, but at last I felt sand under my feet! As that last wave rolled

back it left me on the sand so tired I
could hardly move.

But I knew I could not rest until I

was out of reach of the waves. I got to my feet and made myself run to a big rock. When the next wave came, I held on to the rock. The wave threw me against the rock so hard it hurt me badly. But it did not carry me back to sea. When it rolled back, I was able to run further up on the sand.

The next wave came only to my knees. Before the next one came, I was far up on the sand and came to the grass next to it. I fell down on the grass.

When I had caught my breath, I looked up and thanked God for saving my life. I was tired and hurt and wet. But I was so happy to be alive, I could hardly keep from shouting for joy. I looked out to sea. I could see our ship with the waves still breaking over her sides.

There was no sign of the other men. All of them had gone down in the sea.

Though I had been saved, I still had

many troubles. I was wet and I had no dry clothes to change into. I was hungry and I had no food. I had no gun to shoot any wild beasts to eat, or to save myself in case they wanted to eat me. In short, I had nothing but what was in my pockets — a small knife, a pipe, and a little tobacco, too wet to burn.

It was growing dark. I had to do something right away, because wild beasts hunt at night.

The only thing I could think of was to get up in a tree. So I picked out a thick, bushy one which grew nearby. I saw a little stream, so first I walked to it and drank all I wanted. Then with my knife I cut a big stick. I could use it if I needed to fight.

I then climbed up in the tree and found a place where I could lie back against the branches and rest without falling out. And there I spent my first night.

I Get Back to
the Ship

WHEN I woke up the sun was shining. The storm was over. The wind had stopped. The sea was still.

Much to my surprise, our ship was still above water and was closer to shore than when I had last seen it. The wind and waves must have carried it onto a sandbar near the shore.

I made up my mind to try to swim out to the ship. I must try to get some things that I needed.

The sun was very warm when I climbed down from my tree. I put most of my clothes on the shore in the sun and swam out to the ship.

The ship lay partly on her side on the sandbar. I saw that the part of the ship where the food was stored was dry. I at once found some food, for I was hungry.

I filled my pockets with ship's bread and ate as I went over the rest of the ship. I was very happy to find the ship's dog and two cats still alive and unhurt. I made up my mind that I would try to take them to the land. They would keep me company.

The first thing I did was to make a raft. Many of the big poles to which our sails had been fastened were still on the deck. I cut these poles into shorter pieces with a carpenter's saw that I found. These I pushed over the side. I tied each one to a rope so that it would not float away. Then I let myself down into the water by a rope and I tied the poles together to make a raft. Then I tied this raft to a rope from the ship. But I found when I stood on this raft that it would not carry much weight.

I went back up the rope and took some of the boards that made the floor of the deck. I used them to make the floor of my raft. Then I got three big boxes that had belonged to some of the sailors and put them on my raft.

The thing I needed most was food. I filled one of the boxes with bread, rice, and cheese, and some dried meat.

While I was doing this, I happened to look toward the shore and saw my clothes go floating out to sea. I had not put them far enough away from the water. The tide had come in, and the water had washed them away.

I knew that I needed more clothes. I hunted until I found clothes that fit me. I put them into another of the big boxes.

I found a big box that the ship's carpenter had carried his tools in and lowered it to my raft. I knew that carpenters' tools were worth more to me than gold.

I found two good guns, two pistols, a powder horn, and a small bag of shot. I knew there was gunpowder somewhere, so I did not give up until I found three barrels of it. One was wet, and I did not know how much good it would be, but I took it anyway.

This was all my raft could carry. I called the cats, and put them on the raft. I dropped the dog into the water, and he swam ashore. I had found some oars on the ship, so I used one to paddle with. The sea was calm. The tide was running in. And a breeze blew me toward the land.

Near where I had come ashore the first time, there was a small stream running into the sea. I paddled my raft

into this creek where the water was not so deep.

Here I nearly had another shipwreck. My raft caught fast on a sandbar. By working hard and fast, I was able to get the raft off the sandbar before it upset.

At last I saw a flat place where I thought I could get my raft close to the shore. I paddled as hard as I could and by pushing with my oar on the bottom of the stream, I was able to get the raft close to the land. I held it there by sticking my oar into the sand. As soon as the tide went down, my raft was safely on the land. Then I looked for a good place to put the things I had brought from the ship.

You see, I still did not know whether or not there were other people on this land. If there were other people, I did not know whether they would be friendly or whether they would try to kill me.

Neither did I know what kind of

animals lived here. If there were wild animals, they might try to kill me.

Near where I had landed, there was a hill. I took one of the guns and climbed to the top of it. From that high place, I could see a long way. I did not know whether to be sad or glad about what I saw.

I saw at once that I was on a big island. There were no signs that any other people lived on the island. Far away to the west, I could see two other islands which looked smaller than mine.

There were no signs of wild animals, for which I was very thankful. The trees were full of birds, not like any that I had ever seen. I shot one of them, thinking I would eat the meat. But it had a very bad smell, so I threw it away.

I then came back to my raft and unloaded my goods. This took me the rest of the day. I put the boxes and barrels

in a kind of square around a little space.
I ate some of the ship's bread and cheese
and drank from the stream. I lay down
to sleep in the little square, with my gun
beside me and the cats and dog to keep
me company. I was still very much afraid,
but I was so tired that I was soon fast
asleep. This was the end of my first day
on the island.

I Make Many Trips
to the Ship

WHEN I woke up the next morning, I lay still and thought of what I had to do.

I knew I must make myself some kind of house. I must get more food. The food I brought from the ship would not last long.

Still, I had spent one night without a house. Nothing had hurt me, so the house could wait. I had food for a while too. I had better try to get more things from the ship before another storm came up and broke the ship to pieces.

At first, I thought I would paddle my raft back to the ship. But this was too hard to do. I left the raft on the shore and swam back to the ship. I got on board and found wood to make another raft.

I did not make this one so big, and I did not put so much on it. I found two or three bags of nails, a hammer, an ax, and a stone on which I could sharpen my knives.

I found more guns, more bullets, and more shot. I took all the men's clothes that I could find, a hammock to sleep in, some blankets, and some new sails.

This was all my raft could carry. So I

paddled it to the shore and unloaded my raft near my other things. This took me a long time.

When I had all of my things together, I used the sail to make a small tent. I slept there that night.

The second day had gone fast, as I had worked very hard. But the next days went faster still. Each day, I went to the ship and came back with things I could use.

I took all the ropes I could find, and all the small pieces of sail. While I was hunting through the ship for these things, I was very happy to find more dry food.

Another time, I found some scissors, and some knives and forks. In the captain's room, I found a big bag of money.

This money made me laugh for the first time in many days. It was more money than I had ever seen in my life. But what could I buy with it? I picked it up in my hand and talked to it.

"Oh, money!" I said, "What good are you? I cannot eat you. You cannot keep me warm. You are no good at all!" But still I took it with me.

It had now been thirteen days since I came ashore on my island. If the weather had stayed nice, I would have been able to take the whole ship apart and bring it ashore, piece by piece.

But that very night, I saw big clouds rising in the sky. The wind soon began to blow very hard. The rain fell on my tent, but I was safe and dry inside and I slept well.

When I woke in the morning the ship was gone. Then I was glad I had worked so hard and so fast. The things I had saved off the ship were all I was to have to keep myself alive for many, many years.

Building a Home

I BEGAN to think of making myself a safe place to live. I had not seen any other people or any wild animals. But that did not mean that there were none around.

I knew that I must live near fresh water. I must build a house that would keep out the rain and the heat of the sun. It must be strong enough to keep out wild animals. It should be on a high place so that I could watch for ships.

I walked about my island until I found a place that was just right. It was on the north side of a hill, a little flat place, covered with grass. Since it was on the north, the hot sun would never shine on it too much. Behind it was a wall of rock. If I built my house against the rock, nothing could come at me from behind the house. In front of this rock, the ground was flat for a space and then sloped down to the sea.

At one place in the rock wall, there was the opening into a cave. I made up my mind to build my house right in front of this cave. I drew a half circle on the ground before the rock wall, about ten yards out from the rock and twenty yards across.

Then I cut down many small trees. I cut off their branches and made them sharp at one end. I drove them into the ground on the line I had made. I put them very close together. When they were fast in the ground, they were a little higher than my head.

I put a second row of trees inside the first, and about six inches from it. Between them, I put big ropes that I

had taken from the ship. When it was done, I had a fence that neither man nor animals could get through.

Now I began to carry up all the things I had taken from the ship. The first things I brought up were the sails which I used to make my tent. At that time of the year, it rained very hard and very often. I made a small tent, and then a larger one over it. No rain at all could get in.

In this tent, I put my bed and everything which the rain would have hurt. The other things I put inside my fence. Up until now I had left an opening in the fence so that I could carry things in. Now I closed the opening. Now I was safe.

I made a small ladder. I would climb up the ladder to the top of my fence and stand on the ropes between the

two rows of trees. Then I would pull the ladder up and put it down on the inside. When I had climbed down on the inside, I would take the ladder down after me.

My next work was to make larger the small cave behind the tent. Luckily the rock was soft. Soon I had a kind of cellar for my house.

Once each day, I went out with my gun to hunt. I needed fresh meat. Then, too, I wanted to see what things grew on my island.

The first time I went out, I saw some goats. This made me very happy, for I knew I could drink goat's milk and eat their meat.

The first one I killed was a mother goat that had a little baby goat. The little goat followed me when I carried the mother home. I carried it inside my fence and tried to feed it so I could keep it for a pet. But it would not eat. At

last I killed it and ate it too. This made
me feel very sad.

I often felt very sad. I would have to
talk to myself and try to think of things

that would make me feel happy. I would think of my hard situation, all alone on the island. But then I would think of all my blessings.

"After all," I would tell myself, "you are better off than the other men who were on your ship. They were not saved, and you were.

"And think," I would say to myself, "the ship could have gone down before you got anything. You would have had no gun, no tools, no clothes, no tent. With these things you can keep living for a long time. Maybe a ship will come for you."

Then I would look at my dog and my two cats. It is true they could not talk to me. But they were my friends. They showed in many ways that they loved me. They were a great help to me.

Making the Things
I Needed

WHILE I was making my fence, I was doing other things too. Each day, I went to the highest spot on the island and looked all around. I hoped that I would see a ship.

Just a few days after I came to my island, I cut down a small tree. I made it sharp on one end and pounded it into the ground. I cut another piece and nailed it across the top. On this piece, I cut the words "I came here the 30th of September 1659." Then, each day, I made a little cut. Six of the cuts were the same size but the next one was bigger—to tell me that day was Sunday. The day that was the first of each month, I made

bigger still. I could tell the weeks and months and years.

In my hurry to get things off the ship I had picked up many small things. I found that I had some pens and some ink and some paper. I also found that I had a Bible. There were three or four other books also. I put them all in a safe dry place. If you have no one to talk to but a dog and two cats, it is good to have books to read.

There were also many things which I did not have that I needed very much. I had scissors, but I had no needles, pins, or thread to sew with.

I had an ax and some hammers and nails, but I had no spade to dig with. This had made it very hard to make my fence. I could not dig holes to put my posts into. I had to drive them into the ground, which was very hard work.

I needed a better house inside my

fence. It rained very often, and my tent began to get holes in it. I cut trees and put them against the rock and covered them with branches. But this was not a very big house. It would not hold all the things I had to keep dry.

So I made myself a deeper cave. I had no spade, but I found that the wood of one kind of tree was much harder than the wood of other trees. I took some of this wood and made myself a spade. It took me a long time and the spade was heavy and hard to lift, but it was better than nothing.

The rock was not as hard as I had thought it might be. I used some of the iron I had taken off the ship to dig it loose. Then I found I needed a basket to carry the rock and dirt away in. I had nothing like that, so I made myself a kind of box which I carried on my shoulder.

With my iron bar, my spade, and my

box, I was able to make quite a large cave in the rock. Soon I had it wide enough. Then I worked to the side and out again and came out on the outside of my fence. This saved me the work of carrying each box of rock and dirt up over my fence. I did not make a very large door on the outside. At night I closed the door with rocks.

I worked and worked until I had quite a large cave. It was dark inside, but it was cool and dry.

Then one day when I thought I was almost done, I heard a loud noise. I turned and ran out of my cave as fast as I could. I could hear rocks and dirt falling behind me, but I got out before any fell on me. I waited until I could hear no more rocks falling.

When I went back, there were many big rocks on the floor of my cave and much dirt. I was glad that the rocks had fallen before I had moved all my things into the cave. Now I knew I must cut more trees and make a roof inside my cave.

To make a board, I had to cut down a tree, lay it on the ground, and cut at it with my ax until I had it flat on both sides, and as thin as I wanted it. Each

tree would make one board. I made enough boards to make a roof inside my cave and cut enough posts to hold them up. This took a long time. When the cave was all ready, I moved my things into it.

Now I had time to make some other things. I wanted to sit at a table to eat my food and to read and write.

I had nothing to work with but an ax, a hammer, and some nails. I had saved some boards from the ship and I made a chair and a table. They were not very beautiful, but I could sit at my table the way I had done at home. I used the rest of the boards to make shelves in my cave.

It made me very happy when I had all my things laid out on my shelves. I could see my guns, my nails, my books, and all the things I had saved from the ship. Now I felt that I had a nice, safe, dry place to call my home.

Getting Food

I NEEDED meat. I had to shoot it from day to day as it did not keep long in this warm country.

The goats on my island were very hard to kill. It was hard to get close enough to shoot them. I tried to get my dog to help me. I thought he could get them to come closer to me so that I could have a better shot. But they put down their heads and ran at him with their big horns. He was afraid of them and ran back to me.

I wanted to catch some little ones and keep them until they were no longer afraid of me. The first little one I had would not eat, but later I shot a bigger one in the leg. It could not run, so I carried it home and put it inside my fence. I tied up its leg and it got well. It was not afraid of me. By and by I got a mate for my goat. It was two or three years before I had very many goats. But at last I had enough so that I had goat's milk to drink, and I could kill one for meat if I needed to do so.

What I needed most was something to take the place of the ship's bread and the flour which was almost all gone. I needed food made of grain if I was to stay well.

My cave was big and dry, but it was also very dark. I had no candles to make it light. Candles are made of a kind of fat which gets hard. Fat from the goats would not get hard in this warm country. So I made a little dish of clay and put the fat in it. I needed a little piece of cloth to put in the fat. If I set fire to the small piece of cloth in the fat, it would burn and make a little light.

As I hunted for a little piece of cloth, I came upon a bag in which we had kept grain on board ship. I thought the rats had eaten all the grain that was left in it. I had used the bag to carry other things from the ship to my island. It was just the kind of cloth I needed, but some dust and bits of dirt were in the bag. I took it out and shook it outside the door of my cave.

I thought no more about it until one day I saw some little plants growing beside the door of my cave. They did not look like the grass that had grown there before. I looked at the plants very closely and I saw that some of them were corn plants and some were rice and barley. Those few little seeds must have been left in the bottom of that bag. They had fallen in just the right place to grow.

I took very good care of those plants, you may be sure. I saved every single bit of the grain that grew on them so that I could plant it the next year. It was four years before I had enough grain so that I could eat any. The birds of the island wanted to eat it too, and I had to keep them away. But at last I learned the best way to do things, and I raised enough grain for me to eat.

One day when I went down to the

ocean, I saw a very big turtle. She had come out of the water to lay her eggs in the warm sand. I killed the turtle and carried the meat and the eggs back to my cave. I had had nothing but goat's meat, and the meat of a few birds since I had come to the island.

The meat from the turtle tasted very, very good to me. I baked the eggs in my fire, and ate some. They tasted very good.

It was well that I had those turtle eggs, for that night I became very sick. It was a sickness that men often get in warm countries. First one is very cold. Then one is very hot. I did not have any medicine to take.

I do not know how long I lay there, but I did not die. When at last I was

strong enough to get up, I was too weak to hunt. There was nothing to eat except the turtle eggs. I lived on turtle eggs for many days and at last I was well again.

I made up my mind to walk all over my island and see what grew on it. I did not want to get sick again and have nothing in my cave that I could eat.

Near where I first landed, there was a small stream. I walked up this stream and found many pretty green fields of grass. Some plants grew there that I did not know. But I found tobacco plants there and some sugar cane. Farther up the stream, I found some melons growing on the ground. Grape vines had grown up into the trees and were covered with grapes. They tasted so good that I wanted to eat and eat and eat. But I remembered that once some of my shipmates had eaten too many grapes. They had become sick and died.

I knew that grapes could be dried

into raisins and that they would then keep for a long, long time. I had found something that was of great use to me.

I slept that night in a tree, and in the morning I went farther up the stream. I came to the top of the hill and then went down into a pretty green valley. It was a beautiful place. Wild orange and lemon trees grew here but they had no fruit on them at this time. The lime trees, though, were covered with limes. Every sailor knows that limes are very good for him.

I picked some grapes and limes and put them in a bag I had with me. Some grapes I left on the ground to dry.

When I got home, I found that the grapes were too soft to carry in a bag. The limes were all right, so I made two bags out of sailcloth and went back to the valley for more limes.

The grapes I had left on the ground had been stepped on by wild animals.

So I knew I could not make raisins that
way. At last I found a way to dry them.
I picked the biggest bunches I could
find and tied them to the outside
branches of the trees where they would
be in the sun. I dried more than two
hundred big bunches this way.

Each night when I went back to my cave, I would carry many limes in the bags I had made. It was a long walk, and they were heavy. But I knew the rainy time of the year would soon begin. Then I would be glad to have them.

One day, I found that my grapes were well dried. I carried them home to my cave. It was well that I did, for the next day a big storm came up. The winds blew very hard and my raisins would have all been lost.

The back part of my cave was very cool. There I kept my raisins, limes, and meat. It rained many days but I was safe and dry. I sat at my table and read my Bible by the little light I had made.

The Years Pass By

ONE by one the years went by. Each year I learned more and more. I found that there was no summer or winter on this island. But there were rainy seasons and dry seasons. I learned not to plant my grain at the beginning of the dry season. I learned not to let the rainy season come upon me when I had no food put by, for I could not hunt in the rain.

I learned that if I put branches from one kind of tree into the ground at the start of the rainy season, they would grow and form a thick tight fence. I used these trees to make fences around the fields in which I kept my goats. I made myself a little house of these trees in the valley where the grapes grew. Sometimes I stayed there for two or three weeks at a time in the dry season. It was in that valley that I had my grain fields. The ground was rich and the grain grew well.

I needed some baskets to carry my grain. As a boy, I had watched a basketmaker who used small branches from a willow tree. The trees I used to make my fence were very much like willows. So, one day, I cut some small branches from those trees and tried to make a basket from them. My baskets were not beautiful, but they were very useful. I made plenty of baskets in the rainy season when I had to stay in my cave. But I could not make the baskets tight so that the small grain would not run out.

I found some clay and made pots

which were smaller than the baskets. When they were dry I put one inside each basket. I put straw between the basket and the pot to keep it from breaking. The pots would hold my grain but they would not hold water.

I needed something to carry water in and to cook in. Then one day I saw a broken piece of clay pot that had fallen into my fire. It was bright red and as hard as a dish.

I said to myself, "Well, if they will burn hard like that when they are broken, I will see if I can burn one hard that is not broken." So I made some small pots. I placed a pile of wood around them and set the wood on fire. I kept the fire going for five or six hours and then let it die down slowly.

I could hardly wait till the pots were cool to try them. They were lumpy and thick, but they were hard as could be.

I filled one with water almost before it was cold and set it on the fire. Soon the water was boiling. I put in some goat meat and made some very good soup.

I made some larger pots that I used as ovens. I would build a hot fire on a large flat stone. When the stone was very hot, I would push the fire off it. Then I put my bread on it. I would turn one of my big pots upside down on top of the stone to keep the heat in.

The bread would bake just as if it were in an oven.

Before I could make bread, I had to find a way to grind my grain. The rocks on this island were soft. Little pieces broke off when I pounded my grain on them. These little bits of rock did not taste good.

I cut a big block of the hard, hard wood I had used to make my spade. Then I cut out a place in the middle of it to hold my corn. I pounded the corn with another piece of wood until I had it fine enough to make bread.

In this warm, rainy country, clothes soon wore out. The first things to wear out were my caps. The sun was so hot that I had to cover my head. I made myself a hat of dried goatskin. With the hair on the outside, the rain ran right off it. And it was so big that it kept the sun off me very well too.

When all my clothes wore out, I

made myself a suit of goatskin. I used
a little piece of bone with a hole in it
for a needle. I used a thin strip of skin
for thread.

I also made myself an umbrella. I
cut up many, many goatskins before
I made an umbrella that would work.
I had to find a way to make it let down
so I could carry it under my arm.

By this time I had been on the island eleven years. I was the king of the island. But the only ones I had to rule over were some cats, an old dog, some goats, and a parrot.

My palace was a cave I had dug with my own hands. The table and chair in it had been made by the same hands. I do not think any king would have wanted his people to see him in clothes such as I was wearing. But they suited me very well. I had all I wanted to eat. I had a safe place to sleep. I was alive. For these things I thanked God every day.

A Change in
My Life

ALL the years I was working on my island, I was thinking about the other islands I could see from the top of my hill. Maybe if I could get over to one of those islands, I could then get to the mainland. I could find some other people and ships that would take me home.

Of course, I knew that the people on those other islands might be savages who would kill and eat me. But I thought I would take that chance.

One time, after a storm, I found a small boat had washed way up on the shore. It lay bottom-side up a long way from the water. I worked as hard as I could for three weeks. But I could not move the boat. I even tried to dig the sand out from under the boat. I did get it to turn right side up, but I could not move it to the water.

I then tried to make a boat. I went to the woods and cut down the biggest tree I could find. It was five feet thick and it took me two weeks to cut it down. It took me another two weeks

to cut off the branches and pull them away. It took me four weeks to cut the tree into something that looked like a boat, and three times that long to chop out the inside.

The boat was big enough to hold many men. So I was sure it would hold one man, two cats, and an old dog. Now all I had to do was to get it into the water.

The boat was in a little valley about three hundred feet from the water. I tried but I could not move the boat.

I was very unhappy when I thought of all the work I had done, but I had learned something. After that, I thought a little longer before I started something.

It was another year or two before I tried again to make a boat. This time, I cut down a smaller tree near a little stream. I rolled the log down near the water before I began to work on it.

I made the boat big enough to hold

one man. When it was done, I only had
to dig a small waterway to get it into
the water. I fixed up a little sail for
the boat. I fixed little boxes inside it
where I could put food, water, and
gunpowder so they would not get wet.

I fixed a place to put my big
umbrella so the sun could not shine on
me. Then I took some small trips in
the boat. I was afraid to go very far

until I learned how to make it go where I wanted it to go. But soon I could do that very well.

Then I made up my mind to sail the boat around my island before I tried to sail to the other islands.

I sailed down my little creek and out into the sea. I was only a little way from shore when I felt the water take my boat and start to carry it out to sea. I could do nothing to stop it. There was no wind, so my sail could not help me.

"This is the end of me," I thought as my boat went farther and farther from the island. Soon I would be carried out into the open sea. I would starve even if my boat were not turned over by a storm. I looked back at my island as the most wonderful place in the world.

When the island was almost lost to sight, I felt a breeze in my face. At once I set up my mast and sail. I could still see the island, so I knew how to go. The wind began to blow directly toward it. My boat moved rapidly, going straight ahead of the wind. Finally I got into quiet water near the shore. By that evening, I had reached the land again. I fell on my knees and thanked God for saving me.

My life on the island had been pretty much the same, day after day and year after year. I had now been here fifteen years. I had my two homes, the one in the valley where I raised my grain and dried my raisins, and the first one which I had made when I first came to the island. At each of my homes, I had made fields in which I kept goats so I was never without milk and cheese. I had many baskets of grain in the cool, dry part of my cave. I had found a way

to make the clay pots better so I had all the pots and pans I needed.

One day, I went out for a walk along the shore of my island. I looked down and saw the print of a man's bare foot in the sand!

At once, I was very much afraid. I stopped and looked all around. But I could see no one. I walked up and down the shore trying to find some more footprints. There was just the one.

I came back to look at it again. It was the print of a very large foot. I could see the toes and the heel very well. I knew a man had made it. I was so afraid that I ran for my home.

I got inside so fast that I do not know whether I climbed the ladder over my fence or whether I went in through the hole in the rock. I shut the door in the rock and took my ladders inside.

I did not go to sleep that night at

all! I lay there thinking of all kinds of things and the more I thought, the more afraid I was.

What if the man who made the footprint was hiding somewhere on my island? What if he was a savage who would kill and eat me? What if he found my grain and took it? What if he found my goats and let them all go?

I was so afraid that I did not even think to ask God to help me until I had been in my cave three days. Then one morning when I woke up, I remembered that it said in the Bible "Call upon me in the day of trouble and I will help you."

I began to feel better. That day I went outside again. I took care of my goats. I went to my other house to see that all was well there. You can be sure that I looked all around me as I walked. I was ready at any time to run for my life.

I wished now that I had not made a door through the rock into my cave. I got to work right away. I cut a lot of the trees that grew so easily and made a second fence outside my rock door. I left holes in this fence that I could put my guns through. I fixed my guns so that by firing one and quickly running to the next, it would sound as though more than one man was shooting.

I cut hundreds of branches from this special kind of tree and put them in the ground outside the fence. They grew quickly. Soon they were so thick and strong that no one could get through them unless they knew where to go as I did. The trees hid my home so that no one could see it from the sea.

I also made some new fields for my goats. If anyone found some of them and let them go, I would still have others. This took me a long time, but then I felt safe again.

Cannibals

THE footprint in the sand changed my life in many ways. I got out an old sword and made it very sharp. I never left my home after this without wearing it. I wanted to be ready to fight if I had to. I also wore two pistols which I could stick in my belt; and I always carried a gun. Carrying all of this made me walk very slowly.

Then one day I saw a small boat upon the sea. It was so far away that I could not tell whether it was coming to my island or going away from it. Soon the boat was gone. After that, I always carried a telescope. When I looked through this glass, I could see if a boat was coming to my island. Then I could hide until I found out what kind of men were in it.

One day, I was walking along the shore on the side farthest away from my home, looking for turtles. I saw something that made me stop.

Someone had made a big fire. All around were bones, bones that I knew had come from men. Now I knew what kind of men had been in the boat I saw going away from my island.

They were savages called cannibals. When they had a war, they would capture some of the men they were fighting. After the war, they would have a big feast. They would eat the men they had caught.

I was filled with fear that the cannibals would find out that someone was living on the island. What chance would I have against a crowd of those savages?

I covered the bones with sand. But I

did not forget the cannibals. I thought and thought. What could I do to make them so afraid that they would never come back to my island again?

I thought of putting gunpowder in the sand where they made their fire. But the gunpowder would get wet and would not go off. Then, too, I did not want to use my gunpowder that way. I did not have enough.

Then I thought of shooting them with my gun. I found a place on a hill near where they came ashore. I built myself a little house there. From it, I could see without being seen.

I brought some of my guns there and looked out over the sea. I sat there every day for weeks.

Then I began to think about what I was doing. I said to myself, "You are a man who knows it is not right to kill and eat another man. But these savages do not know that it is not right. Will you be any better than they are, if you kill them for doing something that they think is all right to do? They are not hurting you. You have no right to try to kill them unless they try to kill you."

So I gave up my watching. But I still was very careful to look all around me as I went about my island. I was also careful not to make a big fire that would send up a lot of smoke. Smoke can be seen from far, far away. So I hunted for the kind of wood which did not make much smoke. I found this on a part of the island that I had not looked over before.

I was cutting this kind of wood one day when I saw a place in the rock that looked like the door of a cave. As I had a fire, I took a big stick from it that was burning. It made a little light. Then I took my ax in my other hand and went into the cave.

The cave was not very big but at the

back was another hole. I did not go into that the first day, because my stick did not burn bright enough.

The next day I came back with candles and found that the second cave was a big, cool, dry place. I had need of a place to store more grain and to keep what was left of my gunpowder. I needed a place to keep some of the things I had taken from the ship that I did not use very much but wanted to keep. By moving these things to the new cave, I had more room in my home.

About this time, I had some very good luck. From a ship that had been wrecked on the island in a storm, a barrel of gunpowder had floated to the shore. Nothing else was to be found. Opening the barrel, I found that only the outside of the powder had been harmed. Most of the powder that was inside was still dry and as good as ever. So I had about sixty pounds of good powder.

Three more times, I found bones and saw where the cannibals had had a feast on my island. But they never came ashore on the side where my house was.

More years went by. The parrot I had taught to talk could say many words now. He would sit on my chair at mealtime and talk to me. I always had two cats and one or two little goats that I kept for pets. My old dog had died. But another ship was blown onto the rocks in a storm, and though all the men were killed, a dog got to shore alive. So I had another dog.

I had now been on my island twenty-three years, and I thought I would be there until I died of old age.

Friday

ONE morning when I climbed my fence to look around, I saw five small boats full of cannibals. There must have been about twenty of these savages. You may be sure I got out of sight very quickly. I was most afraid that the savages might wander about the island. If they found any of the work that I had done, they would know that there were people on the island. Then they would not give up until they had found me.

I waited a long time, but I heard nothing. So I climbed up again to look down at the savages through my telescope.

They had made a big fire and had

meat cooking over it. They were dancing around the fire waving their arms as if they were very happy.

Then I saw, off to one side, two others who were not a bit happy. Even as I watched, two of the dancers came over, hit one of them on the head with a big stick, and pulled him over near the fire.

Just at that minute, when their backs

were turned, the other man jumped to his feet and began to run. He was running right straight for my home!

"Oh!" I thought, "what if they all run after him? I cannot fight twenty men all at once!"

Then I saw that only three of the savages were running after him. I also saw that he could run much faster than they could. I had never seen anyone run so fast in all my life.

Between my home and the sea there was a stream. The wild man jumped in and swam across very quickly. He came out on the side near me and ran on very fast.

The three who were running after him stopped when they came to the stream. Two of them jumped in and began to swim slowly across. The other one went back to the fire.

That man was still running straight toward me. I felt that I just could not let him be taken again. I took my guns and climbed over my fence. I came out of the woods between the man and the two who were running after him.

I did not want to shoot because I feared the other savages would hear the gun and come to see what it was. I waited until the two men were very close to where I was hiding. Then I suddenly ran out of the woods and knocked one down with my gun. The other man had a bow and arrow and was getting ready to shoot me. So I had to shoot him whether I wanted to or not. He fell at the first shot.

The poor man who had been running away now stopped. He saw the two wild men on the ground and knew he didn't have to be afraid of them anymore. But he was so afraid of me that he stood there shaking like a leaf.

I called to him. I showed him with my hands that I wanted him to come to

me. He came closer and then stopped.
Then he took another step or two and
stood there shaking.

I talked to him softly even though I
knew he did not know what I was saying.
I smiled at him. Nearer and nearer he
came. Then he fell down at my feet and,
taking my foot, he put it on his head.
This, I thought, was to show me that I
was his master since I had saved his life.

I helped him to his feet and tried to
let him know that I was his friend.

Just then, the savage I had hit with my gun began to move. The man I had saved saw him. He said some words that I did not know. They were the first words I had heard said by a man for twenty-five years, and they sounded good to me. I could see that he wanted the sword which I had in my belt.

I took it off and gave it to him. At once he ran to the other man and cut off his head. When he had done this, he laughed and came back to me. He gave me back the sword.

Then he went to the other dead man and looked at him. He turned him over. He looked first at one side and then the other. The bullet had made a very small hole. It was plain to me that he could not see how the man had been killed. He took the dead man's bow and arrows and gave them to me.

We covered the two dead men with sand. If the others came after them, they could not know the men had been killed.

I took the man to my big cave. I gave him bread and water. Then I showed him the straw covered with skins on which I slept. He lay down and went to sleep.

While he was sleeping, I had time to take a good look at him. He was a very nice-looking man, tall and strong. I thought he might be about twenty-six years old. He had a good face, not cross or mean-looking, but happy and kind.

His hair was long and black. His skin was not black and not yellow and not white, but a kind of light brown. His forehead was high. His nose was about like mine. His lips were thin and red, and his teeth were as white as they could be.

As he lay there sleeping, I thought, "Today is Friday, and today he will begin a new life. I will name him 'Friday.'" And so I did.

My Life with Friday

WHILE Friday was asleep, I went out of the cave and milked the goats.

Soon Friday came out. He came running to me. He was smiling. He tried to show me how happy he was to be alive.

I put my hand on him and said "Friday" to let him know his name. I put my hand on myself and said "Master." I wanted to teach him to speak to me as soon as I could.

I gave him milk in a clay pot and took some myself. I let him see me drink it. He did just what I did. I took some bread and let it get soft in the milk. Then I ate it. He did the same and let me know that he liked it.

Before we went to sleep that night,

Friday could say his name and my name, and "Yes," and "No." He learned very quickly.

We stayed in the big cave that night. In the morning, we started back to my home. When we came to the place in the sand where we had left the two cannibals, he showed me that he wanted to uncover them and eat them.

I let him know that this was very wrong. I looked angry and acted as if I were going to be sick. I took him by the arm and made him come on with me. He walked along with his head down to show me that he knew I did not like what he had said.

When we got to the top of the hill, I looked all around with my telescope. I could see no one on my island. The cannibals had gone. They must have left without looking for the two who had run after Friday.

We went to my home. I gave Friday some clothes. A box full of clothes had come ashore after a ship had been wrecked and some of them fit him quite well. I made him a vest of goatskin and gave him a cap I had made.

I could see by the way he walked that he had never had clothes on before. But he soon became used to them.

I made a place for Friday to sleep in the open place I had left between my two fences. I was afraid at first that he would go back to his old ways. So at night, I made sure that he could not get to me without making so much noise that it would wake me up. I shut my door and took in my ladders and took all the guns and my sword inside with me.

But I did not need to do this. Friday was kind and good. He acted as if I were his father and he a loving son. I do think he would have given his life for me.

I was very pleased with him, and I began at once to teach him everything I could. He learned fast. It made him so happy to please me that he worked very hard.

It was so nice to have someone to talk to and to laugh with, that I, too, was very happy.

I knew that Friday liked to eat meat, so I knew that I must show him that it was all right to eat the meat of animals. After he had been with me three days, I took my gun and took Friday with me to the woods.

I soon saw a goat, with two young ones, lying under a tree. I let Friday know I wanted him to stand still. Then I raised my gun and shot one of the young goats.

Poor Friday! He had heard the sound

of a gun just once before when I had shot the man who had been going to kill me. He did not see that this time the young goat had fallen dead.

He stood there, afraid and shaking. Then he began to tear off his vest to see if he had a hole in his skin, the way the dead man had. He could find no hole, but still he thought I was going to kill him.

I was sorry that I had made him so afraid. But I soon found a way to let him know that I was not going to kill him. I laughed out loud and took him by the hand. I showed him the young goat I had killed and put my finger in the hole in its head where I had shot it.

While he was looking at the goat, I loaded my gun again. I showed him a big bird in a tree. I let him know that I was going to shoot it.

When I was sure he knew what I was

going to do, I shot the bird. It fell to the
ground. Again, Friday began to shake
and talk in his own words. He seemed to
be talking to the gun. I could see that
he thought the gun was magic. I could
not tell him that the gun was not magic
until he knew more of my words.

We carried the young goat home and took its skin off. Then I cut some of the meat and cooked it in one of the pots I had made from clay. When it was cool enough to eat, I took some and gave Friday some. When he saw me eat it he also began to eat. I could see that he liked it very much.

The next day, I roasted the rest of the meat over the fire. Friday let me know that he liked the roasted meat very much. Then he tried to tell me something else.

He tried many ways before I knew what he was trying to tell me. He wanted me to know that he would never eat the meat from another man again. I showed him that this made me very happy.

The next day, I showed him how to pound corn and make bread. He watched me while I baked it too. In a little time, Friday could do everything that I could do. So began the best years I had on my island.

I Teach Friday

NOW I had two mouths to feed. I knew I must plant more grain. So I found more good land and started to fence it in.

Friday helped me. As we worked I told him the names of everything. Before long he could bring me anything I asked for, or go anywhere I wanted him to go. It made me so happy to have someone to talk to. My work was much easier when I had someone to help me. I came to like Friday more and more, because he was so friendly and good.

One day I asked him about his country. I said, "The cannibals that brought you to my island were not your people."

"Oh, no," said Friday.

"Did those men fight better than your people?" I asked.

"Oh, no," said Friday. "We fight better."

"Then why did they have you in their boat?" I asked. "If you can fight better, you should have had their men. They should not have taken you."

But Friday said, "My people fight them in one place and take many men. All our boats at that place. These men come to our island and take just three men and me. Then go away again. No one can help us. All gone other place."

I read to Friday from my Bible. I told him about my country and about my ship, and how we had sailed her over the sea. I took him to the place where she had gone down and showed him the smaller boat from another wrecked ship.

Friday looked at this a long time. Then he said, "We save a boat full of white men from the sea."

"How many men were there in the boat?" I asked him.

He showed me on his fingers. There were seventeen.

"Where are they now?" I asked.

"They live with my people," said Friday.

I asked him if his people had not killed some of the white men, and he said "No, we make them our brothers."

Not long after this, I took Friday to

the top of the highest hill. It was a clear day and we could see an island far away.

Friday began to jump around and to dance. I could see he was very happy. He pointed to the island and said, "There my country. There my people live."

I said, "Friday, would you like to go back to your own country?"

"Yes," he said, "I be glad to go to my own country."

"What would you do when you got there?" I said. "Would you be a savage again and eat other men?"

"No, no!" he said, shaking his head. "I tell people how grow corn, eat goat meat, and drink milk."

"Will they not kill you then?" I asked him.

"No, they will not kill me. They like to learn," said Friday.

Then he told me that they had learned many things from the other white men they had saved.

"I will let you go if you want to go back," I said. Friday smiled and let me know that he could not swim that far.

"I have a boat," I said, "and I will give it to you."

"I go if you go," he said.

"I cannot go. They will eat me," I said.

"No, no! I will not let them eat you," said Friday.

I thought about those other white men on his island. Maybe if we could get together we could think of a way to get to the mainland.

The next day I took Friday to the place where I kept my boat. I did not have a sail on it anymore, but Friday could paddle it very well.

Then I said, "Well now, Friday, shall we go to your island?"

"Oh, no!" said Friday. "This boat much too small." So after we had paddled awhile, we came back to shore.

I said, "We will make one just like this

and you shall go home in it." I meant that we should both go, but he did not understand me. I thought this would make him very happy, but he did not say one word. He just stood there with his head down, looking very unhappy.

I said, "What is the matter, Friday?"

Then he said, "Why you not like Friday? What me done? Why you send me home?"

I said, "I am not angry. I thought you wanted to go home. I thought that would make you happy."

"Yes," said Friday. "We both go. No wish Friday there, Master here."

I took his hand and said I would never send him away as long as he wanted to stay with me.

A Rescue

FRIDAY and I began to make a big boat that would carry us over the sea to his island. When the boat was ready, we cut some smaller logs and put them under it. These rolled like wheels. We had to go very slowly, but at last Friday and I pushed our boat down to the sea.

Friday could make that big boat go wherever he wanted it to. I asked him if he thought he could take it over the sea.

"Yes," he said, "I could take it over the sea very well, even in a big wind."

It was now time for the rainy season. I knew we should not try to go very far in our boat at this time of the year. We made a place in our stream where we could tie up our boat and keep it safe.

Soon after this, Friday was out on the shore looking for a turtle to cook for our dinner. I heard him coming back. He was running as fast as he could. He came up over the fences almost as if he were flying.

"Oh, Master!" he cried. "Oh, Master! Bad, bad!"

"What is it, Friday?" I said.

"Out there on the sea," cried Friday. "One, two, three boats . . ."

I loaded all my guns and my pistols. I put on my big sharp sword. I gave Friday some guns and the ax. Then we went over the fence.

There were three boats on the shore. I could see twenty-one cannibals. There were three men whose hands and feet were tied.

Telling Friday to keep close behind

me, I went through the thick woods I had planted to hide my home.

We went as quietly as we could. Soon we were at the edge of the woods nearest the cannibals.

They had killed one of the men and were ready to kill another. The third man was one of the white men Friday had told me about that had come to his island in a boat.

I turned to Friday and said, "Now, Friday, do just as you see me do!"

I put down two of the guns I had been carrying. Friday did the same.

I lifted a gun and when I saw that Friday had his lifted also, I said, "Now, fire at them!" We both shot at once.

Friday did better than I did. The cannibals were all close together and he killed two and hurt two more. I killed one and hurt two. But the surprise did almost as much to hurt them as our shots did. They did not know what to do.

They did not know anything about guns.

Friday kept his eyes on me and did just as I did. I lay down the gun I had shot and picked up another.

"Are you ready, Friday?" I said.

"Yes, Master," said Friday. We shot again.

Two more savages were killed, and many more were hurt.

Now they were all running here and there, calling loudly, falling down and getting up again and running into each other.

"Follow me, Friday," I said, picking up the other gun.

Friday picked up his last loaded gun and followed me. If he was afraid anymore, he did not show it.

We ran out of the woods toward the cannibals, calling out loudly. I ran to the poor man they had been going to eat. As I ran, I could see some of the cannibals getting into a boat. I called to Friday to shoot them, and he did. He killed two more and hurt another.

I cut the vine around the poor man's hands and feet. He could hardly stand. I had a bottle of wine in my pocket and I gave him a drink. He started to talk in words that I had heard in Spain.

I said, "We cannot talk now. Fight if you can," and I gave him my sword.

This seemed to put new life into him. He put an end to two or three cannibals right before my eyes.

Three others had pushed off in one of the boats and paddled off as fast as they could. They were the only ones of the twenty-one savages who got away.

Taking my guns, I ran with Friday to their boats. Friday started to push a boat out into the water. But when I stepped into the boat, I saw that there was a man on the floor. He was tied, hands and feet. He was an older man, and he looked as if he were more dead than alive.

I cut the vines that held him and lifted the poor man's head. I called Friday to come and tell this poor man that we would not hurt him.

At the sound of Friday's voice, the man opened his eyes. He sat up in the boat.

Friday ran to the side of the boat. He

took the older man in his arms. He kissed
and hugged him and cried for joy. Then
he jumped out on the sand and danced
and jumped about like one of my little
goats, all the while making loud, happy
noises. Then he ran back to the boat,
took the older man's head in his arms
again, and talked with him in their own
language. The tears ran down their faces.

It was some time before I could find
out who this man was, but at last Friday
told me. It was his father that we had
saved from the cannibals.

Soon the wind began to blow and a big storm came up. The waves were so high that we were sure the three cannibals who got away could not have reached their island in their little boat.

We had to get our two friends to our home. They could not walk. They needed food and water. I had just a little bread and some raisins in my pocket. I gave these to Friday and he gave them to his father. Then he ran toward our home.

In a few minutes he was back. He had a clay pot full of water and some bread. We gave water and bread to the white man too. When he had eaten that, I gave him some raisins.

Friday then took the white man on his back and carried him down to the boat. He put him in beside his father. Then he paddled the boat up our little stream as far as he could go. I walked on the shore.

My Family

I HAD thought once before of my being the king of my island. At that time, it seemed very funny because I had no one but a dog, two cats, and a parrot to rule over.

Now I was king of three other men! I had saved the life of each one, and they all seemed to think very highly of me. But I found that a king has many things to think about.

First, Friday and I had to bury the dead savages. We did not want anything left on our shores that would show what had happened there.

We took good care of Friday's father and the other man. We fed them on goat soup. They liked this very much and soon were strong again.

The other man was from Spain just as I had thought. I had been to his country. I could speak and understand his words, so I could talk to him.

I could not talk to Friday's father except through Friday. I would tell Friday what I wanted to know. He would talk to his father in their language. Then he would tell me what his father said.

I asked Friday's father if he thought the cannibals who had gotten away would bring back others to fight us. Friday's father said he thought their boat would not get through the storm that had come up as they left. But even if it did, he thought they would be so afraid that they would never come back. They knew nothing about guns. They would think that Friday and I had magic that could kill men.

When the savages did not come for

a week or two, I began to think again of going to Friday's homeland. Friday's father told me again and again that his people would all be good to me.

The man from Spain said Friday's people did not have enough food. And they had nothing to cook it in if they had had food. They did not have any guns or powder or shot. He said he knew they would do anything for me if I came and gave them food.

This gave me much to think about.

The grain I had put by would be just enough for the four of us if we were careful of it. But it would not be nearly enough for all of Friday's people and all of those white men. We talked it over. We thought it would be better for all four of us to get ground ready to plant, and to plant every bit of grain we did not need to keep us fed. Then, when we had enough grain to feed the other men, we could go and get them.

We made new fields and planted all of the grain we could. We caught more goats. When the grapes were ripe we dried so many that I think we could have filled many barrels.

Of course, we had to make more baskets now and bake more clay pots.

Friday and his father cut down trees and made boards from them. I wanted to have them ready to build a bigger boat when the time came.

Our grain grew very well. We brought over four hundred baskets full of grain into the big cave. That was plenty to feed us and all the men from Spain. It was plenty to take with us on our ship if we wanted to try to get to the mainland.

Now I had enough food for everybody. I decided to let Friday's father and the man from Spain go back to their island for the other white men who were there.

I told the man from Spain that he should bring no one who would not promise to do just as I would tell them to do. The men must promise not to fight us or hurt us.

I gave them one of the boats the cannibals had brought them over in. I gave them each a gun and powder and shot. But I told them not to use it unless they had to. We put into the boat food and water enough for them for many days, and food for their countrymen to eat on the way back.

I gave them a piece of sail on a stick. They were to hold it up when they came back so that we would know them, and not take them for a boat full of cannibals.

A Ship from England

FRIDAY and I waited for Friday's father and the man from Spain to come back. They had been gone eight days.

So I was not surprised when Friday came running in one morning crying, "Master, they come, they come."

I jumped up at once and went out to see. A boat with a sail on it was coming to our shore, and coming quite fast. Much to my surprise it was not coming from the north where Friday's island was, but from the south.

I called Friday in quickly and told him that these were not our friends. Then I went in and got my telescope.

I was only halfway up the hill when

I saw a big ship out in the sea. It was a ship from England, my home.

I was very happy to see a ship from my home country, and yet something seemed to tell me to take care. Why would a ship from England be in this part of the world? Ships from England did not often come here. There had been no storm to drive it here. So I hid myself and watched the ship through my telescope.

A small boat came to the shore and eleven men got out. Three of them had their hands tied together. One of these three fell on his knees and lifted his hands to the other men as if he were begging for something. The other two sat on the sand with their heads down as if they had given up.

Friday was with me now. "Look," he cried, very softly, "your countrymen eat other men too!"

"No, no!" I said, "they may kill those three, but you can be sure they will not eat them."

They did not kill the three men. They left them sitting there on the sand and began to walk over the island to see what kind of place it was.

They were gone quite a long time. When they came back the tide had gone out and their boat was sitting on the sand, a long way from the water. They knew they would have to wait for the tide to come in again. It was getting very hot. They all went up into the woods. I thought they might go to sleep.

The three men whose hands were tied were sitting under a big tree. Friday and I came up in back of them.

"Who are you?" I called.

They jumped up and turned to look at us.

"Do not be afraid," I said. "Tell me quickly what I can do for you."

One of the men said, "Am I really talking to a man, or did God send you from heaven to help us?"

"I am a man from England just like you," I said, "and I want to help you. This is my man Friday. We have three guns each. Now tell us your story quickly." As I talked, I untied their hands.

"I will make it as short as I can," said the man. "I am the captain of that ship. One of these men is my mate, and one is a friend who was on my ship. My men have turned against me. They were going to kill us until they saw this island. Now they are going to leave us here to die."

"Do they have more than the one gun?" I asked.

"They have two," he said. "One of them is still in the boat."

"Well, then," I said, "if you will help us, we can fight them. I think they are asleep. Would you like for us to kill them all? Or shall we take them alive and tie them up?"

"There are only two real bad men among them," said the captain. "If those two were taken, I think the other men would be all right."

"Can you tell me which ones they are?" I said.

"Not so that you would be sure you had the right men," said the captain. "But I will fight by your side, and I can tell you when I see them."

We went back into the thick woods. Then we stopped.

"Sir," I said to the captain, "if I can help you, will you do something for me?"

"Anything, anything!" cried the poor man. "I will do anything you say. I will take you wherever you want to go if we get my ship back again."

"Well," I said, "there are only two things that I ask. First, if you stay on this island you must do as I say, and second, if we get your ship, you will take me and my man home to England."

He said he would do these things, and gladly.

"Then," I said, "here are guns for you. Now, what do you think we should do?"

As we were talking, we heard some of the men calling to each other. We walked to the edge of the wood and saw two of them.

Just then, one of us made some noise and the two men cried out to the others, who came running out of the woods. The mate and the captain's friend fired their guns at the leaders.

One of them fell dead. The other was badly hurt and a second shot finished him.

The other men gave up. They said they would give up their bad ways and follow the captain's orders again. He said he would not shoot them. However, we tied their hands together and put them in my big cave.

The Captain and I

THE captain and I told each other our stories. Then I took him and his two friends to my home. There I gave them food to eat and milk to drink. I showed them the things I had made. Each thing was a new surprise to them, and we talked for a long time.

I thought we should think of ways to get back his ship. He said there were twenty-six men still aboard. They all knew that they could be hanged for turning against their captain. So he did not think they would give up without a fight.

We heard a shot from the ship. This was to tell their men to bring the boat back to the ship. No boat came in answer to their shot. So another boat left the ship and came toward the shore. We went back to the edge of the woods.

There were ten men in this boat. They all had guns. The captain looked through my telescope at them. He said three of them were good men who were afraid of the others.

When they came on shore, they called as loudly as they could. No one answered.

Three of them stayed in the boat. Seven stayed close together and walked into the woods. They came out at the top of the hill above my house. Then they just turned around and started back down to their boat.

I had Friday and the mate go over to the little stream. They called loudly but kept out of sight.

The men from the ship were just getting back to their boat when they heard Friday call. Seven of them jumped out and ran toward the sound. Of course, they came to the stream. They called to the men in the boat to come up the stream and take them over.

When they were all on the other side, they left only two men in the boat. Meantime, the captain and I had crossed the stream farther up so that we were now on the far side.

As soon as the other men were out of sight, we surprised the two men. The captain knocked one down with his pistol. The other, who was one of the good men, gladly gave up to the captain.

Friday and the mate were leading the other men through the woods by calling first from one place and then from another. Friday and the mate came back to us pretty soon, tired and hot. But it was three hours before the others gave up hunting for their friends and came back to the boat.

When they got back, they found the two men gone. The tide had gone out again, and their boat was aground.

They called the names of the two men, ran here and there, and sat down to rest. Then they did the same things over again.

It was now nearly dark. We could have killed them one by one if we had wanted to kill, but the captain wanted to kill only the bad leaders.

So the captain and Friday took their guns and went nearer to the men. One of the leaders and another man walked away from the others and came close

to where the captain and Friday were hiding. The captain and Friday stood up and shot them.

When we heard the sound of the guns, the rest of us ran up and joined the captain. I told the good man who had been taken from the boat, whose name was Robert, to call out to them.

He called to them one by one. "Tom Smith, Tom Smith," he called, "throw down your guns or you will be killed."

"Who is with you?" asked Tom Smith.

"Our captain, and fifty men," called Robert. "Give up at once!"

"Will we not be killed if we give up?" called another.

Then the captain himself called out, "You, Tom Smith, you know my voice. If you throw down your gun at once, you will all be saved, all but Will Atkins, your leader."

When he heard this, Will Atkins cried out, "Why are you going to kill me, and not the others? They are as bad as I!"

"That is not true," said the captain. "It was you who thought of all this. But if you give up, I will talk to the governor about it, and see if he wishes to save your life." By the governor, he meant me.

The men threw down their guns. When they were all tied up, my "big army of fifty men" came out of the woods. I kept one man with me and did not come out. I thought it was best for them not to know how their governor looked.

Now the captain talked to the tied-up men. He told them that any sailor who turns against his captain can be hanged. The men all begged him to save their lives.

The captain said he would try to save them, that is, all but Will Atkins. The governor had said he must die.

The captain walked back to where I was hiding with the rest of my army, one man. I thought we could now get these men to help us get back the ship but that we could do nothing more tonight.

We did not think we should put Atkins in with the other men. We untied Atkins's feet and those of two more of the men and took them up to my house. The mate and I took turns watching them all night.

The captain and Friday took the others to the big cave. Then they lay down and slept there.

We Take the Ship

IN the morning, the captain and Friday called the men out of the cave. The captain told them that their lives had been saved last night only by the kindness of the governor of this island. He said that when they got back to England they would all be turned over to the law and hanged.

"However," he said, "if you will help me get back the ship, I will try my best to save you when we get back home."

Of course, the men all said they would help him. They fell on their knees and told the captain they would follow him to the end of their lives and do whatever he asked of them.

"Well," said the captain, "I will go talk to the governor. I will tell him what you say."

He came back to me and we talked it over. The captain thought he could believe in these men, but we wanted to be very sure. Also, we did not want them to know that we did not have a big army to back us up.

The captain went back to the men. He told them that he would only take five of them to help him. The governor would keep the others here. If any one of them did something he should not do, then the governor would have the others shot right before their eyes.

Now we began to get ready to take the ship. There was the captain, the mate, and the captain's friend, the two good men who had helped us last night, the two I had kept in my home last night, and the five the captain picked from those who had spent the night in the cave.

Friday and I stayed on the island to watch Atkins and six other men.

The captain made his friend the master of one boat, with four men in it, and he was master of the other, with his mate and five men in it.

They did not start until it was very dark.

The first boat came close to one end of the ship. The captain took his boat to the other end. Robert was in the first boat and he called to the watchman. The watchman and another man came and Robert talked as long as he could. He told the watchman how long they had had to hunt for the first boatload of men, and so on.

The captain and his men, by this time, had climbed up the anchor chain and were on the ship. They came up behind the watchman and the other man and hit them on the head with their guns and tied them up. Then they let down a rope ladder and the other boatload of men came on board.

They soon had everyone on deck tied. Then they fastened the doors so that the men sleeping below decks could not get out.

The captain told the mate to break down the door of the room where the man who now called himself captain was sleeping. But that man had heard the noise and was ready for them with a gun in his hands.

When the mate broke down the door, he shot the mate in the left arm, but the mate shot him in the head.

The rest of the men gave up and no more lives were lost.

As soon as everything was safe, the captain had seven guns fired from the ship. This told me that they had taken the ship and that all was well.

Friday was asleep at the door of the cave and I had been sitting on top of my hill, watching, ever since they left. I was very tired and lay down right there and went to sleep.

The next morning, the captain brought some meat and some vegetables, some sugar and biscuits ashore. But better than these, he had brought me some shirts, some shoes, and a suit of clothes.

We took them to my home. We cooked the food and ate. I put on the clothes. They felt very queer and tight after my loose goatskins, but I was very glad to have them.

After this, I went to the cave, opened it, and called Atkins and the other men out. I told them that I was the governor of the island and that I was going back to England with the captain. I said that the captain would take them back to England if they wanted to go, but that, of course, we would have to turn them over to the law when they got there, and they would no doubt be hanged.

But, I said, if they wanted to, they could stay on my island. They all said they would rather stay here than go back to England to be hanged.

Then I took them over my island. I showed them my house and all that was in it. I took them to my valley and showed them where I planted my grain and where the grapes grew and how to dry them. I showed them how to make bread and how I took care of my goats and how to make cheese. In short, I told them all that I had learned in the long years I had been there.

I left them five guns and a barrel and a half of powder. I said I would have the captain give them two more barrels of gunpowder, some shot, and some garden seed, which I had often wished I had.

I left them then, and Friday and I went on board ship to spend the night.

The next morning, two of the men came swimming out to the ship. They said they would rather take their chances with the law than to stay on that island with Tom Atkins. After some time, the

captain let them aboard. They turned out to be very quiet, hard-working fellows who made no more trouble.

When the tide came up, I went ashore in the boat with the things I had said I would bring to them. I left a letter for the men from Spain who might be coming back with Friday's father. I told them that if I could, I would send a ship to take them off the island.

Then I left my island for the last time.

I took with me my goatskin cap, my umbrella, and my parrot. I also took the money I had had no use for all these years. I knew I could use it now.

It was the 19th of December 1686. I had been on the island twenty-eight years, two months and nineteen days.

And so we set sail for my home at last.